CAT SECRETS

Jef Czekaj

SCHOLASTIC INC.

ISBN 978-0-545-85229-6

Published by Scholastic Inc., 557 Broadway, New York, NY 10012,
by arrangement with Balzer + Bray, an imprint of HarperCollins Children's Books,
a division of HarperCollins Publishers. SCHOLASTIC and associated logos are trademarks
and/or registered trademarks of Scholastic Inc.

12 11 10 9 8 7 6 5 4 3 2 1   15 16 17 18 19 20/0

Printed in the U.S.A.   40

First Scholastic printing, February 2015

Typography by Carla Weise

For Felix the boy, Keira the girl, and Tucker the cat. –JC

This means that if you are a:

Especially if you are a mouse . . .

Hey, you!
Yes, you!
You don't look much
like a cat!

LEAP

If you *absolutely,*
really, truly are a cat,
let's see you take
a nap!